The Dirty Old Teddy

The toys in the nursery listened in horror. The dirty old teddy – who they loved so much – was going to be thrown away!

REPRINTED 1990

Enid Blyton's
The Dirty Old Teddy

Once there was an old, old teddy bear in the toy cupboard. He was so old and dirty that nobody knew what colour he had once been, and he didn't even remember himself.

He only had one arm, and one of his legs was loose. His eyes were odd, because one was a black boot button and the other was brown. He had a hole in his back and sawdust sometimes came out of it. So you can guess he was rather a poor old thing.

But he was wise and kind and loved to make a joke, so the other toys loved him and didn't mind him being so dirty and old.

"All the same, I'm afraid he'll be thrown away into the dustbin one day," said the panda, shaking his head. "I'm afraid he will. He really is *so* old and dirty."

The little girl in whose nursery the bear
lived never played with the old teddy.
She had a fine new one, coloured blue,
with a pink ribbon round his neck, two
beautiful eyes, and a growl in his
middle. She loved him very much. She
always pushed the old teddy away if he
was near her.

One day her nurse picked up the old teddy and looked at him. A little sawdust dribbled out of the hole in his back.

"Good gracious!" said Nurse. "This old teddy really must be thrown away. He isn't even nice enough to be given to the jumble sale."

"Well, throw him away, then," said Joan. "I don't want him. He looks horrid with only one arm and a leg that wobbles, Nurse. I never play with him now."

All the toys listened in horror. What! Throw away poor old teddy! Oh dear, what a terrible pity!

"Well, I'll put him in the waste paper basket when the maid brings it in," said Nurse. She put the teddy on the table beside her and went on with her knitting. Soon the bell rang for dinner, and Nurse forgot about Teddy.

As soon as she had gone out of the room the toys called to the bear, "Hurry, Teddy! Get down from the table and hide at the back of the toy cupboard!"

The bear fell off the table and limped over to the toy cupboard. He really was very frightened.

He hoped that the nurse wouldn't remember she had left him on the table. She didn't remember—because when she came back she had another child with her, besides Joan. A little boy clung to her hand, and Nurse was talking to him.

"You will love staying with us, Peter
dear. You shall play with Joan's toys,
and have a ride on the rocking horse."

Peter was Joan's cousin and he had come to stay with Joan for three weeks. He was a dear little boy, but very shy. The toys watched him all the afternoon. He was frightened of the rocking horse because it was so big. He liked the doll's house because everything in it was little. He loved the top that spun round and played a tune, and he liked the train that ran on its lines.

When bedtime came, and he sat eating
bread and milk in front of the nursery
fire, he began to cry.

"I've left my old monkey behind," he wept. "I always go to bed with him. I shall be lonely without him."

"Well, you shall have one of Joan's toys
to take to bed with you," said Nurse,
and she took him to the toy cupboard.
"Choose which you would like, Peter."

Peter picked up the panda—and then the rabbit—and then the sailor doll—and then the blue cat. And then, quite suddenly, he saw the dirty old teddy bear looking up at him out of his odd brown and black eyes. He gave a squeal and picked him up.

"Oh, Nurse! Can I have this darling soft teddy? He looks at me so kindly—and I do like his funny eyes. Oh, please, please, may I take *him* to bed with me?"

"Good gracious! It's the bear I meant to throw away in the dustbin!" said Nurse. "You don't want a dirty old toy like that, surely!"

"Yes I do—yes I do!" cried Peter, and he hugged the bear hard. "I shall cry if you don't let me have him."

"Of course you shall have him, but if you love him so much I shall have to mend him a bit tomorrow," said Nurse. So Peter took the old teddy to bed with him—and you simply can't imagine how happy the bear was!

He cuddled up to Peter and loved him.
It was such a long, long time since he
had been taken to bed by anyone. He
was so happy that even his little growl
came back when Peter pressed his
tummy.

And next day—good gracious! Nurse took him and made him a new arm. She sewed on his wobbly leg. She mended the hole in his back—and she made him a beautiful blue suit with little sleeves!

You can't think how different he looked! The other toys looked at him in amazement and joy. "You won't go into the dustbin now, Teddy," they said. "You look simply lovely!" And he does, doesn't he?